SHELTERWOOD

Susan Hand Shetterly
Illustrated by Rebecca Haley McCall

Tilbury House, Publishers • Gardiner, Maine

When I was a girl, people in town said that Milton Mallett's woods were one of the finest sights in the whole county. From the windows of his house on the hill, he looked past the field and down to the trees that grew straight to the river.

In October the leaves of the hardwoods turned copper, orange, red, yellow, and purple. Pines and spruces towered above them.

In winter the hardwoods were bare. The pines and spruces held snow on their branches.

"No one knows trees like your grandfather does," people told me.

Every Sunday my grandfather drove
into town in his old blue pickup, and
my mother fixed us a big supper.

One evening in early spring, he said
that the owners of the land around his
were cutting all their trees down. Day
after day chain saws ripped. Tree after
tree snapped and fell. It made him sad,
he said, to hear it.

"It's as if they thought they were
cutting hay," he said.

My grandfather was a logger and cut trees, too, but my mother and
I knew he never made the mistake of thinking trees were hay.

He folded his napkin, set his hands flat on the table, and said, "I'd like to teach you about trees, Sophie. My woods will be yours some day, and I don't know anyone else who can show you how to take care of them but me."

"What do I need to know?" I asked.

"Everything we can think of," he said.

I glanced at my mother.

"Would you like to do that?" she asked.

"Yes, " I said.

"Why don't you plan to take Sophie to stay with you when school's out? Teach her then?"

"That sounds good," he said, turning to me to see what I thought.

"May Alistaire come, too?" I asked.

My grandfather gave me a big smile. "He's always welcome. You know that." Alistaire was my coon cat who slept at the foot of my bed at night.

My grandfather got up from the table and went into the hall and put on his wool coat and his old wool hat. My mother kissed him good night on the cheek, stretching up on the tips of her toes.

On the last day of school he came to get me in his pickup, and I moved with Alistaire from my house in town to his house on the hill. In bed in the little room in the attic, Alistaire lay at my feet as we listened to the wind whistle through the trees.

I remembered the story my grandfather told me about his grandfather who stacked logs on the river bank in the winter. When spring came and the ice melted, the high water rushed the logs away to the sawmill faster than a girl or a boy could run.

I remembered the story of my grandfather helping his own father stack logs on a sledge when he was a boy. A pair of oxen pulled it out over the snow pack.

"They were the gentlest animals," he told me. "And when they pulled, their breath hung in big clouds around their faces."

A deep echoing sound rose up the hill. I opened my eyes with a start. The room was pitch dark. The wind had stopped. I tiptoed downstairs and sprinted into my grandfather's bedroom.

"Grandpa!" I whispered. "Someone's outside!"

He sat bolt upright. We both listened. It came again: "Whoooo.... Who. Who. Whoooo...."

My grandfather laughed quietly.

"It sounds like a great horned owl to me," he said. "That bird has a nest in a pine close to the river. I imagine it's getting ready to hunt mice."

"Whooooo...," the owl said again.

My grandfather shut off his alarm clock.

"Now that you're up," he said, "why don't I take you out to see the woods before sunrise?"

"Don't be scared," I told Alistaire, but he was sound asleep as I hurried into my jeans and jacket.

"Dress warm!" my grandfather called.

"I am!" I called back.

We stepped outside. A sliver of moon hung in the sky. My grandfather pointed to a dark shape skimming just above the field. It flapped twice, then coasted away down across the hill. I slipped my hand into my grandfather's hand.

We hiked to a camp he built years ago by a little pond. At the broken window that looked over the water, we drew up two chairs and sat down. Nothing happened. My chair began to feel chilly and hard. Then, one by one, five tall shapes moved out from the trees.

My grandfather put a finger to his lips, and we watched the deer stretch
their necks to drink. The sky lightened. A wood duck splashed down, raising
a little furl of silver water. The deer slipped away through the trees and a
winter wren landed on the windowsill.

"Sometimes I can't help asking myself who owns
these woods," my grandfather said. "Oh, I've got the
written deed to the land—but who do the woods really
belong to? Me? Those deer? That old owl out by the
river who keeps asking, 'Who?'"

On the way back to the house we knelt in a boggy
part of the road to touch the hoof prints of a moose.

"Are there bears here, too?" I asked.
"There are bears," he said.

One afternoon I noticed that the noise of chain saws from the land next to my grandfather's woods had stopped. I climbed up to the ridge to take a look. The people were gone. Stumps sprawled over the ground, and rain was beginning to cut into the bare topsoil.

It made me sad to see it.

On Sunday, I told my mother about the moose prints and the owl and the deer.

"How many deer were there?" she asked.

"Five," I said.

"Will you teach me the names of the trees and how to tell them apart?" I asked my grandfather.

"That will be a pleasure," he said.

We made sandwiches and poured lemonade into a thermos and took them with us to the woods.

My grandfather picked some leaves from a sugar maple and some from a red maple, and showed me the differences in shape—how the sugar maple leaf has softer, rounder cuts and edges.

We brushed our hands down the trunk of a spruce tree. He wanted me to feel the scaling of its bark.
"You can learn this tree by touch," he said.

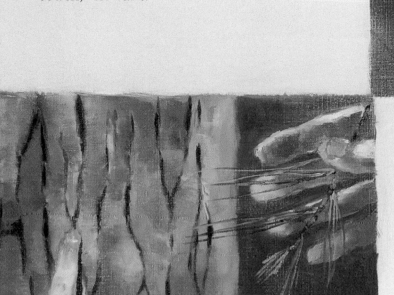

He showed me the furrows in the bark of the old white pines, and how five needles grow from each tight cluster.

We found where red squirrels had ripped strips of woolly bark from the cedars to line their nests.

"What kind of tree is that?" I asked, pointing to a pale green one that looked especially soft.

"It has trouble making up its mind," he said. "See its little cones and the needles? In that way, it's like other softwoods. But in the fall it loses its needles as if it were dropping leaves like an oak or a maple."

"What is its name?" I asked.

"People have trouble making up their minds, too, I suppose. Some call it hackmatack, some say larch or tamarack. Which name do you like best?"

"I think hackmatack's the best," I told him.

We sat with our backs against an oak and ate the sandwiches and drank the lemonade. Warblers were moving through the branches overhead making quick, sweet music. My grandfather closed his eyes, and I sat listening to him breathing, and to the voices of the birds.

I could see down the woods road a distance to where it curved up along the hill again. Suddenly, a big animal ambled out onto the road. Its snout was a light tan color, and its fur was thick and very black—a bear!

I watched it sniff the air in every direction. Then it shuffled along the
road, made a quick little jump that surprised me, and vanished into the
woods. As fast as it had appeared, it was gone, and all I could hear was my
own heart beating.

When my grandfather woke up, I didn't tell him about the bear right away.
It was too fresh and special in my mind. Later, when I did tell him, he said,
"You're lucky. I've only seen a bear twice in these woods, and I've lived here
all my life."

At sunset we headed down to the river. My grandfather wanted to show me the glow of the yellow birches in the last light of the day.

He taught me that a young red spruce needs shade to grow strong and straight.

Young maples and firs need some shade, some sun.

A white pine needs all the sun it can get at its top, but you mustn't allow too much light to fall on its sides. If you do, it gets branchy.

Big trees protect the small ones until the small ones grow up.

"It's called a shelterwood," my grandfather said.

One day we drove in the pickup to the pulp mill where trees are turned into paper.

"What can I do for you, Milton?" the manager asked.

"This is my granddaughter, Sophie. We've come to find out what you're paying for wood these days."

Then we drove to the sawmill that turns logs into boards, and asked them what they were paying.

On the way home we stopped at Fern Torrey's Ice Cream Shop. My grandfather pulled out his pencil and pad. We figured that we would get the best price for a load of maple, which would be sawed into boards to build houses and furniture, and even, my grandfather said, to make violins.

"Tomorrow we'll set out a skidder trail in the maple stand" he said.

"What'll you have, Sophie?" Fern asked.
"Banana split, please," I said.
"And you, Milton?"
"Same," he said.

We looked for the wind-firm trees, the tallest and the biggest. They were the trees my grandfather would not cut.

"They know how to bend in the wind," he said. "When we cut away the trees around them, they won't blow down. They'll drop seeds and start a new generation."

We tied orange ribbons to the trunks of the trees my grandfather planned to cut. Then we chose the bumper trees for the logs to bounce against when he twitched them out of the woods with the skidder. We tied blue ribbons around them.

I worked with my clippers. My grandfather worked with his chain saw. We cleared a trail between the bumper trees and laid the branches and the brush over it so that the skidder treads would not tear up the ground.

The next day my grandfather cut the maples. He limbed them, topped them, twitched them free, loaded them onto the log truck, and drove them to the sawmill.

When I walked back to the stand, it was raining. The branches of the big trees moved in a slow wind. The woods smelled sweet and moldy.

Rain fell on my hands and face and in my hair as I pulled the cut limbs away from young trees and laid them evenly over the ground. Some I piled together to make safe cover for rabbits and nesting places for grouse and winter wrens and other birds. Given time, insects would eat the branches, and they would eventually rot down.

Whenever I found a small tree, I snipped a space around its trunk with my clippers. I made sure it had room, and enough light and shadow to grow, so I could come back when I was grown and find it here.

Tilbury House, Publishers • 2 Mechanic Street #3 • Gardiner, Maine 04345 • 800-582-1899

Text copyright © 1999 by Susan Hand Shetterly
Illustations copyright © 1999 by Rebecca Haley McCall

First printing: October, 1999   10 9 8 7 6 5 4 3 2 1

Library of Congress Cataloging-in-Publication Data
Shetterly, Susan Hand
Shelterwood / by Susan Hand Shetterly : illustrated by Rebecca Haley McCall.
p.   cm.
Summary: While staying with her grandfather in his house in the woods, Sophie learns about the different kinds of trees and enjoys the beauties of the natural world.
ISBN 0-88448-210-3 (hc : alk. paper)
[1. Trees Fiction. 2. Forests and forestry Fiction. 3. Nature Fiction.
4. Grandfathers Fiction.]
I. McCall, Rebecca Haley, ill.. II. Title.
PZ7.S55455Sh 1999
[Fic]--dc21   99-12470
                                                     CIP

To Ken—SHS
To Rob—RHM
With special thanks to Betty and Mel Ames of Atkinson, Maine.
Illustrations by Rebecca Haley McCall, Blue Hill, Maine.
Design and layout: Rebecca Haley McCall, Jennifer Elliott, and Geraldine Millham.
Editorial and production: Jennifer Elliott and Barbara Diamond.
Color transparencies: Ken Woisard, Blue Hill, Maine.
Color scans and film: Integrated Composition Systems, Spokane, Washington.
Printing and binding: Worzalla Publishing, Stevens Point, Wisconsin.